THE WIND IN THE WILLOWS

by KENNETH GRAHAME

#4 Home Sweet Home

Adapted by Laura Driscoll

Illustrated by Ann Iosa

Sterling Publishing Co., Inc.
New York

Library of Congress Cataloging-in-Publication Data Available

10 9 8 7 6 5 4 3 2 1

Published 2007 by Sterling Publishing Co., Inc.
387 Park Avenue South, New York, NY 10016
Originally published and copyright © 2004 by Barnes and Noble, Inc.
Illustrations © 2004 by Ann Iosa
Distributed in Canada by Sterling Publishing
^c/o Canadian Manda Group, 165 Dufferin Street
Toronto, Ontario, Canada M6K 3H6
Distributed in the United Kingdom by GMC Distribution Services
Castle Place, 166 High Street, Lewes, East Sussex, England BN7 1XU
Distributed in Australia by Capricorn Link (Australia) Pty. Ltd.
P.O. Box 704, Windsor, NSW 2756, Australia

Printed in China
All rights reserved

Sterling ISBN-13: 978-1-4027-3296-6
          ISBN-10: 1-4027-3296-1

For information about custom editions, special sales, premium and
corporate purchases, please contact Sterling Special Sales
Department at 800-805-5489 or specialsales@sterlingpub.com.

Contents

The Smell of Home

It was a cold December evening.
Mole and Rat were on their way
back to Rat's house.
They had been out all day,
having fun with Otter.
Now they were tired,
cold, and hungry.
They hurried home
as fast as they could.
Then suddenly,
Mole stopped in his tracks.

4

Sniff, sniff.

Mole's nose twitched.

What was that smell?

Why, it smelled like…home!

It was *Mole's* home!

Mole had not been home
in a long time,
not since he had met Rat
and stayed to live on the river.
Mole wanted to see his house.
He *had* to! He just *had* to!

"Ratty, wait!" Mole called out.
"Come back! Quick!"

When Rat heard the news
he knew what they had to do.
"We are going to find
your house!" Rat said.

So Mole followed his nose.

Rat followed Mole—

across a ditch,

through bushes,

and over a field.

Then Mole disappeared...

into a hole in the ground!

Mole's House

Rat followed Mole
down the hole
and through a tunnel.
At the end was a door.
It was the door to Mole's house.
Mole was so happy to see it!

Then Mole opened the door,
and he was not happy anymore.

Inside, it was very dark,
very cold, and very dusty.

"Oh, Rat," Mole cried.
"Why did I bring you
to this poor, cold little place?"

Rat was not listening.

He was running here and there,

lighting lamps and looking around.

"What a nice little house!" Rat said.

"I'll build a fire.

You can dust.

We'll have this place

in order in no time!"

Rat was right.
Soon there was a warm fire
in the fireplace
and the whole house
was clean and tidy.

"What about dinner?" said Mole.
"I have nothing to feed you."

Rat smiled at Mole.

"Don't be silly," he said.

"We'll find something."

Rat was right again.
When they looked in the
cupboards they found
sardines and crackers.
Then they found
sausage and mustard.
Rat even found
four bottles of cider.

"It's a feast!" said Rat.

They sat down to eat.

Guests

Just then, Rat and Mole
heard voices outside
Mole's front door.
"It's the field mice," Mole said.
"They come and sing
every year at this time."
Rat jumped up from the table.
"Let's go see!" he said.

What a sight it was!
Outside were ten little mice,
smiling and singing.

Mole smiled too.
It was just like old times
to hear them again.

"Beautiful!" cried Rat
when they were done.
"Now, come in and
warm up by the fire!
Have something hot to drink!"

"Yes, come in, come in," said Mole.
Then he remembered.
"We have nothing to give them!"
he said to Rat.

Rat fixed that.
He sent the oldest mouse
out to buy some treats.

Then he warmed some cider
over the fire.

Soon they were all very warm,
very full, and very happy—
especially Mole.

Good Night

When the meal was done
and the mice were gone,
Rat yawned a big yawn.
"Mole, I'm tired," Rat said.

He told Mole good night.
Then he climbed
onto Mole's sofa.

Mole was tired, too.
So he climbed into his bed.
He put his head down
on his pillow.

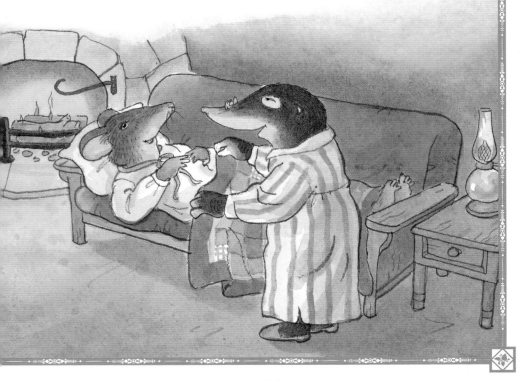

Mole looked around his house.

He smiled.

It was plain.

It was simple.

It was small.

It was all his own, too.

Mole loved living with Rat.
He looked forward to
going back to the river,
but it was good
to know his house
would always be there
to come home to.